This igloo book belongs to:

....

Contents

igloobooks

Published in 2018
by Igloo Books Ltd, Cottage Farm, Sywell, NN6 0BJ
www.igloobooks.com

WKT001 1018
2 4 6 8 10 9 7 5 3 1
ISBN 978-1-78670-732-1

Written by Stephanie Moss
Illustrated by Paul Nicholls

Designed by Justine Ablett
Edited by Stephanie Moss

Printed and manufactured in China

Knight Stories

igloobooks

A Surprise for Norman

When Norman woke up on his birthday, he couldn't wait to celebrate with his friends. They always had **amazing** birthday banquets for everyone and Norman knew the knights would plan something special for him, too.

In the castle courtyard that morning, Norman's friend,
Charlie, hurried over.

He's come to tell me about my birthday treat!

thought Norman.

Can you help me clean out the horses?

asked Charlie, instead.

Had Charlie forgotten Norman's birthday? Norman was disappointed, but he wanted to help, so they **scrubbed** and cleaned the **smelly** stables.

Yuck! cried Norman.

Charlie **chuckled** to himself and gave a secret smile.

6

When they had finished,
Gwen appeared, looking
very pleased to see Norman.

*Maybe she's come
to wish me a
happy birthday?*

thought Norman.

Can you help me clip
my dragon's toenails?

asked Gwen, instead.

Gwen seemed to have forgotten Norman's birthday, too, but he helped her straight away.

You're such a good friend,

said Gwen.

When Norman finished clipping he cleaned the dragon's ears, as Gwen **giggled** to herself.

8

Norman's **boring** birthday chores didn't end there. Whenever he finished one, another knight appeared and asked for something else.

Norman hoped each time that someone would remember, but things only got worse.

It wasn't just the knights who had forgotten Norman's birthday, either. The princess asked him to polish the windows at the top of the **tallest** tower and the king wanted Norman to count all of his gold coins!

Norman felt **exhausted**. Even though he hadn't celebrated his birthday, he was happy he had spent it with his friends. Suddenly, Charlie appeared holding a **big** box.

Can you help me open the door?

11

Norman stepped into the Great Hall and he couldn't believe his eyes.
There was an **amazing** birthday party inside, good enough for the
king himself. Norman saw jesters, jugglers and even a **huge** feast.

Norman smiled. His friends hadn't forgotten his birthday after all!

You're such a good friend that we wanted to give you the best surprise party ever!

said Charlie.

13

Tournament Trouble

Every year the king held a grand tournament. All the knights wanted to win the trophy and trained hard for the events. But one year, the king was nowhere to be seen.

Where is he?

thought Charlie.

Then, the royal trumpeters announced the princess onto the stage. She said the king had dragon pox, so she was hosting the tournament instead.

My events will be a little bit different,

she giggled.

The knights felt nervous. What did the princess mean? Then it was time for the joust. It was Charlie's best event, but he couldn't believe it when the princess swapped his lance for a **fluffy** feather duster!

I can't win with that silly thing,

thought Charlie,
feeling cross.

The first knight to tickle their
opponent until they fall on the floor
laughing is the winner!

announced the princess.

Charlie didn't want to give up, so he did as the princess said.
His first opponent was Millie, but she was so good at
tickling, he started **laughing** straight away.

That was fun!

said Charlie.

And the fun didn't stop there.

There were custard pies instead of arrows in the archery competition.

Wilbur the wizard lent them magic wands for their sword fight.

They even played hide-and-seek with the ghosts!

Everyone **laughed** and **cheered** each other on. By the end of the day, they had forgotten about winning the old events. Then, it was time to present the trophy.

And the winner is...

began the princess...

... You!

cried Charlie.

The princess had made all the tournament events so much fun that nobody needed the trophy any more. The crowd cheered for the princess. **Hip-hip-hooray!**

21

The Bravest Knight

The new knight, William, was really brave and everybody was talking about it.
When the others were scared, he was the first to race to the rescue.
But something strange happened each night. William disappeared!

How did you become so brave? asked Ned, one evening.

It's almost like magic, gasped Gwen.

William just smiled and took a sip from his cup. Then he **sneaked** out of the Great Hall as usual.

The next morning, the knights heard **shouting** from outside the castle walls. The guards lowered the drawbridge and frightened villagers ran inside.

A mountain giant has escaped!

He's destroying our homes!

24

The knights had never seen a
mountain giant before.
As it got closer, they felt scared.
STOMP-STOMP!

William can help,

said Ned.

But this time, he was
nowhere to be found.

The knights searched the castle, until they heard a
CRASH-CLINK from Wilbur the wizard's secret tower.

When they looked inside, they found William,
searching through empty bottles of bravery potion.

William explained that everyone in his old kingdom used to laugh at him for feeling afraid.

I took the wizard's potion every night so I could feel brave, but now it's all gone.

Gwen smiled.

You might have needed magic at first, but it was really brave to tell us the truth all on your own,

she said.

Then, Ned told William all about the mountain giant.

28

If only we could think of something to scare him away,

said Ned.

Then, William had an idea.

I'm really scared of ghosts. Maybe the giant is, too?

he said, looking nervous.

Ned and Gwen thought William's plan was really clever, but they had to protect the villagers from the giant. So they left William to climb the **spooky** tower all on his own to ask the ghosts for help.

William felt really scared, but the friendly ghosts helped straight away.
They flew out of the window, making **scary** noises.
The terrified giant ran away and everyone cheered.

You really are the bravest knight,

said Ned.

The Great Crown Quest

Ned and Millie were two of the king's **best** knights, but they were always arguing. One day, he called them both into the throne room.

I'm sending you on an important quest,

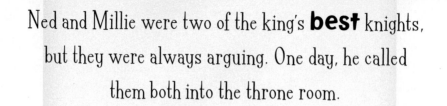

he said.

The princess had lost her crown and it had to be returned before the royal procession.

I'll find it first, boasted Millie.

No way! said Ned.

They both headed in different directions to look for it.

Millie searched the castle from top to bottom.

She **climbed** up the tallest tower...

... and **dived** into the castle moat.

But she still couldn't find the princess's missing crown anywhere.

Ned looked for the crown in
every pot in the kitchen...

... down every secret
passageway in the castle...

... and even in the royal lavatory. Soon, he ran out of places to look, too.

The knights were wondering what to do next when they **bumped** into each other in the courtyard. Suddenly, they both spotted the crown at the bottom of the old well.

There it is! they cried together.

They both tried hard to reach it, but the crown was too far down.
At last, they realised they couldn't complete their quest alone.

We'll have to help each other,

said Millie, and Ned agreed.

37

Ned asked Cook for her **biggest** pot to tie to the rope.
Millie **climbed** in and Ned turned the handle to lower her
down the well. Soon he heard her call from the bottom.

Got it!

When they returned the crown to the princess, just as the procession was about to start, the princess was overjoyed.

I knew we could rely on you to work together,

said the king.

39

Goodnight, Dragon

Lucy loved her cute new baby dragon, Albert, but there was just one problem. He refused to go to sleep every night. He made so much **noise**, all the other dragons had to cover their ears.

Albert kept everyone awake all night... even the king!
By breakfast time they could hardly keep their eyes open.

Whoever makes that dragon fall asleep tonight can have ten pieces of gold!

declared the king.

That night, people came from all over the castle to tell Lucy their ideas. They all wanted to be the one to succeed and make Albert fall asleep, but nothing anyone tried seemed to work.

First, Wilbur the wizard came to see Lucy.

My sleeping potion will send your new dragon straight to sleep,

he said.

Albert **gulped** it down, but he **spat** it right out again!

43

Everyone knows
that tickling a
dragon's toes sends
him to sleep,

said Charlie.

So he tried exactly that.
Then he **tickled** him all
over! But Albert just
giggled and was more
awake than ever.

44

Blacksmith Betty tried building
Albert a comfy new bed.

Norman told him the
longest bedtime story
he could think of...

... while the jesters played
a sweet lullaby.

But Albert **still** wouldn't go to sleep.

45

When it was nearly morning, everyone was ready to give up, except for Lucy.

I suppose I could try one last bedtime story,

she yawned.

So she settled down next to Albert and began to read.

46

Lucy was so tired that soon, she felt her eyes begin to close. It wasn't long before she drifted off to sleep. Albert smiled. With Lucy sleeping beside him, he felt warm and safe at last.

Albert had been too afraid to sleep on his own all along. Thanks to
Lucy, he finally fell fast asleep. The castle was quiet and there
wasn't a sound... for a few hours, anyway!

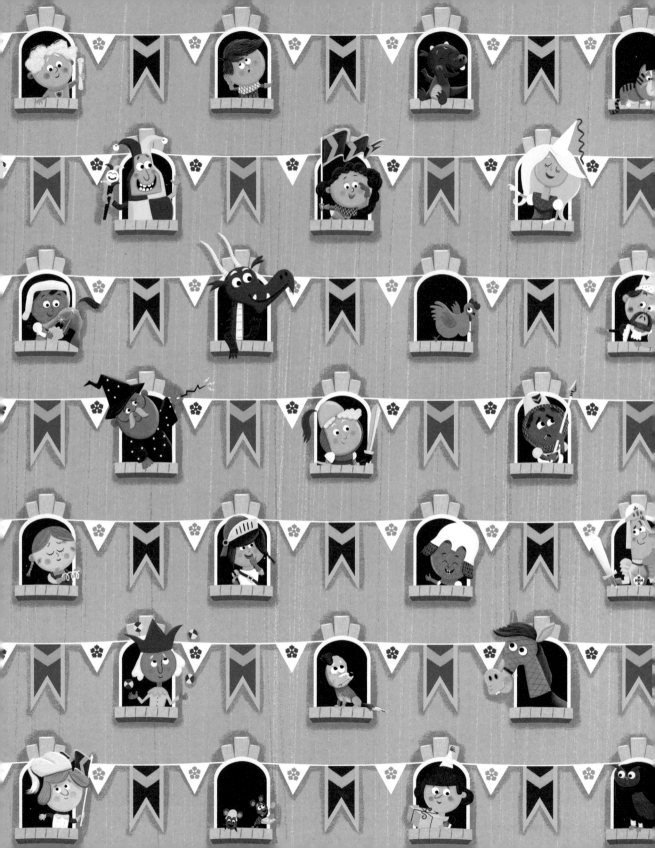